TREMORS FROM THE FAULTLINE

TREMORS FROM THE FAULTLINE

TAMARRA KAIDA

AFTERWORD BY SUSAN E. COHEN

VISUAL STUDIES WORKSHOP PRESS · ROCHESTER, NEW YORK · 1989

We tell ourselves stories in order to live.
Joan Didion, *The White Album*

Partial funding for this book was provided by
the Office of the Vice President for Research
at Arizona State University and the School of
Art Research Incentive Grant.

Visual Studies Workshop
31 Prince Street
Rochester, New York 14607

Making Sense
Just Like in the Movies
Crazy People
The Vegetarian
Awakening

■

Accident
Daydream
Motherhood
Father and Daughter
The White Porsche
A Good Father
Birthday Party
Lucky Man
Ex-Wife
Malice
Artifacts
Family Ties

■

Revelation
Legacy
Eden
Reckoning
Boogieman Blues
John Updike
Housecleaning
Nantucket
Hawks

Making Sense

One summer, while she was in a country that was not her own, she found she could no longer separate dreams from reality. This troubled her since she knew she wasn't crazy and needed to make sense of her experiences. But as her experiences became less credible her ability to assimilate them diminished proportionately.

Everywhere she traveled she encountered unusual people who made marvelous offers. A woman promised to teach her to fly if she would forget everything she had ever known. An old man said he could foretell her future, then laughed mysteriously, and revealed nothing. A beautiful child told her never to grow up or she would certainly die.

Every night she dreamt she was in a house filled with an intense and holy light. She yearned to remain there forever. Yet every morning she was sent from this house into the phantasmagoric world with the admonition that she must make sense of things.

Just Like in the Movies

She wanted to be a fashion model and dressed like one. He had recently appeared in a Pepsi commercial and auditioned for a part in a daytime soap opera.

They met in Central Park while jogging. A week later they started living together. He said it was love at first sight. She smiled in agreement.

For two months they were perfectly happy until she discovered she was pregnant. He behaved as if it were all her fault and assumed she would get an abortion. She was appalled by his attitude. They had their first fight and said terrible and true things to each other. He stormed out. She cried all night.

At dawn, he returned, took her in his arms, and asked her to marry him. They kissed as the camera moved closer.

Crazy People

Some days she was so anxious, she found herself muttering desperate, halfhearted prayers before she left her apartment and ventured onto the street. There were good reasons to be frightened. Crazy people were everywhere: on the subway, in the elevator, at the office, on the television, in the newspapers.

At breakfast she watched a newscast which told of a group of men who had raped a woman on a pool table while their friends cheered. The woman, evidently, had entered the bar only to buy cigarettes. Finishing her coffee, she turned off the T.V., wondering if the raped woman had quit smoking.

On her lunch hour she read about a man who had lost his job, fought with his wife, and then massacred most of the people in a southern California MacDonald's restaurant. An eleven year old boy tried to escape on his bicycle but the killer got him anyway. The child's father was quoted as saying, "I told him before about riding his bike all over the place. I told him he shouldn't do it, that there are crazy people out there." She wished the kid had listened.

After work she stopped at a discount drugstore to refill her Valium prescription. She also bought a large bottle of Tylenol which she carefully examined for possible tampering.

The Vegetarian

For a long time she could not remember what had actually happened. The police said she had shot him twice, once in the chest and once in the head. It was the second shot—the one to the head—which finally stopped him.

In a way, he had asked for it by taunting her ceaselessly, calling her "stupid" and "veggie-brained." On that Sunday he had been drinking heavily and by evening was feeling mean and looking for a fight. The children were at her sister's but were expected back for supper. She boiled water for spaghetti and continued to ignore his attempts to start a quarrel.

In drunken frustration he ran out to the backyard yelling "I'll make you listen to me." He stumbled back with two of the children's baby ducks in his big hands. "How about duck soup? I'll make duck soup for the happy family!" He dangled one of the squawking ducklings over the pot of boiling water. She screamed at him to stop. Having caught her attention, he laughed and let it drop. Scalding water splashed out of the pot. In the midst of the commotion she ran for the hall closet and returned with the little handgun he had bought for her to protect herself.

He was holding the second duckling over the bubbling pot and laughing maniacally. She made her choice.

Awakening

She told him that she suspected she didn't really exist, because when she closed her eyes she vanished and only thoughts remained. Someone else's thoughts.

Exactly how this happened was unclear to her. It was difficult to explain, but she was certain someone else was making up everything. Life was only a movie and she was an actress playing herself—as she had many lifetimes before. She said she finally understood that life was serious but not exactly real in the way she had once believed.

He looked at her as if she were crazy.

Accident

Standing in the shower on Monday morning she discovered a lump the size of a robin's egg in her left breast. On Wednesday she went in for tests. By Friday the doctor had confirmed her worst fears. Though no one was waiting for her at home she was anxious to reach the safety of her bedroom before considering the surgery he recommended.

On the freeway she found herself trapped behind a collision. All around her people left their vehicles and ran toward the accident. Numbly she sat and stared at the distant ambulance lights. From the radio in the empty car beside hers she heard about a town that had been smothered in mud when a volcano erupted. Thousands were reported dead. She could scarcely breathe.

Mesmerized by the revolving lights and surrounding violence, she reached inside her shirt and touched the contaminated breast as if it were a sick and needy child. Drifting into memories of past loves she continued to caress herself until, overwhelmed, she came with cries of loss and pain.

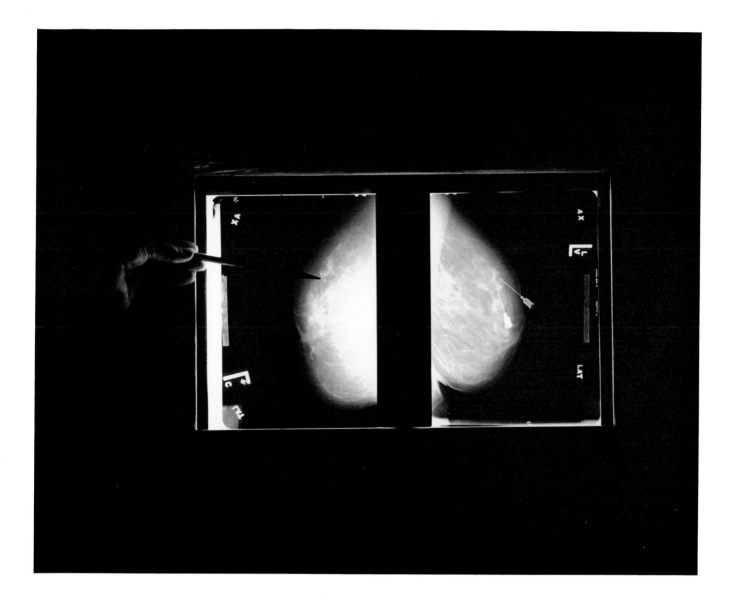

Daydream

Sometimes she envied crazy women: the ones who had stopped trying to make sense of things and did as they pleased; wild women free of husbands, children, money and God; ladies without makeup, resisting domestication and believing their own truths. These crazy women were not like her mother who, declared schizophrenic by men with degrees, did exactly as she was told and lost her mind.

Motherhood

It seemed easier when the girls were little. Then all she had to do was see to their physical well-being and to love them. True, they took a lot of her time and prevented her from pursuing her own interests. She felt compensated by the knowledge that for her, motherhood was the primary profession.

Lately it was becoming more difficult. The telephone rang incessantly inviting one or the other of her children to covert remarks and flirtatious giggling. She sensed their fascination with the mystery of their transforming bodies. Their awkward beauty and secretiveness recalled her own adolescence. She began to dread the inevitable.

Father and Daughter

Although they disagreed on many issues and argued vehemently about politics, she went home as often as possible just to be with him. Secretly she enjoyed the excitement of these verbal battles and, to her mother's dismay, instigated discussions on imperialism at the dinner table.

All of her life he had been a distant man absorbed in books and shielded by a melancholy no one could pierce. Nevertheless, she admired his dour wit and liked the fact that he was a gentleman who wore a jacket and tie, even in the house, where only his wife would see him.

In her opinion he was still handsome, despite the toll liquor and illness had taken. She knew he had affairs, and sometimes she tried to guess which of her parents' friends was his current mistress. This curiosity wasn't born of jealousy or malice but from the desire to understand what, if anything, brought happiness to a man like her father.

The White Porsche

Three days after her sixteenth birthday she wrote a note saying she was leaving for good, and stuck it to the refrigerator with a smiling-face magnet. "Have a nice day, Bitch!" she shouted at the empty kitchen, then slammed the door shut. Defiantly, she took the white Porsche, knowing that by the time her mother returned from the women's tennis tournament, she would be at her father's house in San Diego. He wouldn't make her give it back since he hated her mother even more than she did. If he didn't let her stay with him she would head for Hollywood and become an actress. Everyone said she was pretty and took after her father. He had been on the stage when he was younger and she decided she had untapped acting ability. Bolstered by visions of stardom she drove confidently into the western desert toward California.

Her mother returned earlier than expected, having lost another match. She had already decided to send her daughter to boarding school when she read the note and breathed a sigh of relief. After all, a Porsche was a small price to pay to be rid of a tiresome and difficult daughter.

A Good Father

Even though he was on vacation with his family, twin boys and a red-haired wife, he managed to call her every day. He told her he loved her more than anyone.

On the rare occasions she wasn't home he left messages on her machine. Before she met him she would have considered these X-rated. Now she replayed them just to hear his voice.

In their last conversation he told her that his wife accepted him as he was and didn't interfere in his life. He said he would not leave his family in order to marry her because his sons needed a good father.

She explained that she wanted more from him than an affair, that she was thirty-three years old and wanted to have a baby.

He said he saw no reason why that couldn't be arranged.

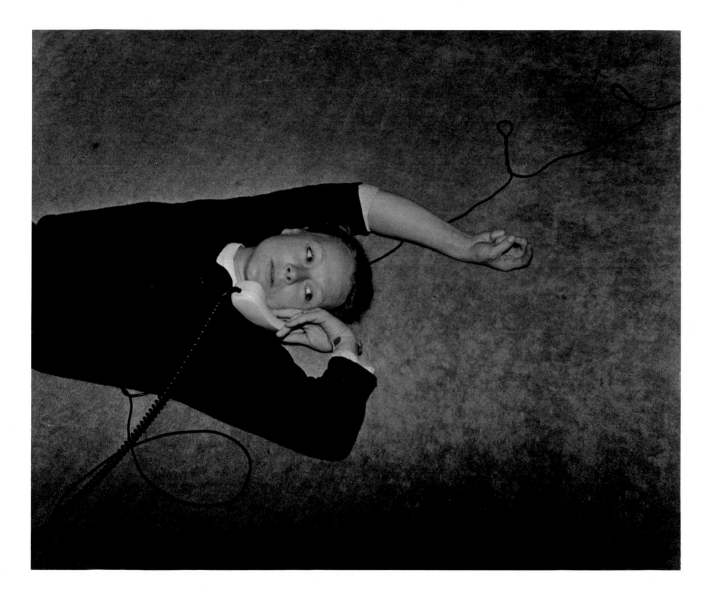

Birthday Party

In his search for the perfect relationship he loved and left many women, always believing the next one would save him. On his fiftieth birthday he dreamt he came home and found all of them living in his house. They seemed comfortable with each other and oblivious to his presence.

He felt like a ghost.

For a while he watched them cook, clean, wash each other's hair and bathe the children he had abandoned long ago.

He envied their easy contentment.

Finally, he summoned enough courage to ask his third wife why they were all there. She looked at him incredulously: "Just because you left each of us doesn't mean we'll ever go away." And they all laughed.

Lucky Man

Until recently he would have described himself as a fortunate man, someone who had achieved most of his desired goals. He had challenging work, enough money, and two grown sons, both of whom loved and admired him. Remarkably, he still loved the woman he had married thirty years earlier. People liked him.

By all accounts it was a good life.

Yet he wasn't satisfied and couldn't say why. He had a nagging sense that somehow he had missed out on something important. Often when he was driving alone he found himself looking for an exit which would take him into another life—something altogether different.

Then it occurred to him that perhaps death, the thing he had always feared, was the ticket for such a journey.

Ex-Wife

It made her angry to think of him with that woman until she realized that eventually his sweet young bride would desire babies. Since he wasn't very good at saying "No" to a pretty face, he would comply.

It pleased her to imagine him, at his age, struggling with diapers and strollers, his lust domesticated by a joint checking account.

Cheerfully, she poured another glass of wine and savored the knowledge that life would dole out its own brand of justice.

Malice

Although they were no longer on speaking terms, she thought of him more often now than when they were living together.

It infuriated her that he claimed so much of her attention. Despite valiant efforts to have nothing to do with him, she was rarely free of his insidious presence.

In the shower, images of him with his pretty mistress appeared before her tightly shut eyes, making her scream obscenities until she grew hoarse. Not a night passed in which he didn't disturb her fitful dreams with lewd suggestions.

What was it that enabled him to invade her mind any time of the night or day, like an incubus determined to torment his hapless victim, then act as if nothing had happened when he chanced to meet her on the street?

How could she prove she knew he was trying to drive her crazy?

Who would believe a jilted woman?

Artifacts

After he left, she read and re-read love letters he had written to her, in the hope that she might discover what made love die. It was hard to believe that the ardent words, once so impassioned and still firmly embedded in sheets of paper, were no longer true.

Gradually she realized the letters were a mystery in themselves, relics of a vanished faith. Evidence but not explanation. Like pottery shards and dinosaur bones they were testimony to something greater which once was.

Family Ties

After twenty-eight years their marriage was ending, almost, it seemed, of its own accord, like some appliance that could no longer be repaired.

He was in love with one of his students. She with her boss. They were eager to divorce and remarry.

This would have been relatively simple had they not had so many children. The oldest was no problem for she was married and lived in California. Their sons were out in the world, one traveling in Europe, the other practicing yoga with a guru in Oregon. They would understand.

The youngest, unfortunately, was still at home. A sullen fourteen year old suffering from acne, shyness and menstrual cramps. This unhappy child had become a painful reminder of their flawed union. Indeed, she was keeping them bonded against their wills with her hysterical fits and attempts at suicide.

Despite themselves, they couldn't stop being mommy and daddy.

Revelation

During her seventh year the purpose of life was revealed to her in a dream. She understood that the world was a big classroom where everyone had come to learn something they considered important. Only they often forgot what that was. Amnesia was necessary since each person had to discover what really mattered or the lessons of life were useless.

It was explained that many wonderful and some terrible things would happen to her as she grew older. But she should not believe too much in the events themselves, for like the movies, they were illusions. Rather she should try to perceive them as opportunities for learning what needed to be known.

Already a serious student, she asked if at the end there would be an examination.

"Yes," replied the voice in her head.

"What if I fail?"

"Then you can repeat the lesson. There is no hurry."

When she awoke she knew someone had told her something very important except it was in a foreign language.

Legacy

Surrounded by family and friends, she stood poised before her birthday cake and sensed that at last the spell would be lifted.

Thirty-eight tiny flames attested to the fact that she had outlived her mother by one full year. They proved that she was stronger than the inadvertent curse left upon her by a distraught woman whose last words were: "You wait and see how hard it is to just live."

For years she had harbored a secret dread that somehow she was destined to follow in her mother's footsteps.

Taking a deep breath, she made the wish, then blew out every candle.

Eden

One morning, in the midst of dressing for work, she realized she couldn't face another day. Her will felt completely spent, so she stopped the ritual preparations and went back to bed.

World weary at 7:00 a.m.

It wasn't that she wanted to die but rather to enter another realm, where living didn't hurt so much, where kindness reigned and love could be counted on.

Another reality altogether.

She inserted the tape into her Sony Walkman and closed her eyes. Soon a soothing voice supported by the gentle sounds of a rolling ocean was instructing her to take a deep breath and relax. Gradually she let go of thoughts and found herself in a spendid garden of exotic flowers and beautiful trees. Brilliantly colored birds welcomed her. A soft breeze stirred the fragrant air. Harmony prevailed.

She was home again, if only to visit.

Reckoning

Even though she wasn't old and had good health, she could feel the years were tipping the scale in favor of the past. It was plain that now there were more memories than potentialities.

And fewer people left to love.

They were dispersing one by one, each with good reason and some regrets, impelled by some inner force like migrating birds calling and crying across the winter sky.

All she could do was stand and watch.

It was becoming clear that vigilant attention would soon be required, for she understood that all things, especially the most ordinary, needed to be acknowledged, even praised, simply for being, or they too would pass as indecipherably as life itself.

Boogieman Blues

On the bad nights she awakened at four o'clock knowing what would happen next. Occasionally she was able to listen to her husband's gentle breathing as if to a wordless lullaby and return to sleep, but often demons captured her attention. Then, like dwarfs performing a pantomime, her anxieties transformed themselves into absurd certainties, convicing her the worst was immiment.

Imprisoned by fear she lay in the dark praying for the black sky to turn a reasonable gray.

John Updike

One night she dreamt John Updike had agreed to become her lover. She made the proposition on the golf course near the third tee. At first he was taken aback by her request but after scrutinizing her for a full minute, he blushed slightly and said, "Well, why not. Yes, I suppose so."

He continued his game and she followed along, occasionally chatting with him about the weather and golf. Intermittently she told him about herself. By the eighth green he had his arm around her shoulders and they were laughing comfortably. Anyone looking at them would have assumed they had known each other for years.

She admired his writings. He liked her no-nonsense approach to life and love. In his room they made love passionately and perfectly. She loved the wetness of his mouth and felt as if she were drinking him into herself. He asked if she were a witch. "No," she said, "but I know a little about the magic of dreaming."

Housecleaning

One day while vacuuming the bedroom floor she noticed portions of the rug disintegrating before her eyes. The vacuum cleaner was pulling up decomposing carpet as though it were ancient parchment or mummified skin.

Undaunted, she persisted in her task, clearing away rotting wood and cracked cement until she hit dirt—hard-packed, yellow dirt embedded with jagged stones protruding like broken teeth. Shuddering, she continued pushing the roaring machine back and forth, sucking up dirt and pebbles with each stroke. Brown dust was everywhere. "This is mining of another kind," she said to no one in particular. "Eventually I'll reach the core."

When the dense earth gave way to deep caverns, she hesitated. Beneath her feet lay a vast and malevolent darkness.

Incited by dread, she began to pray.

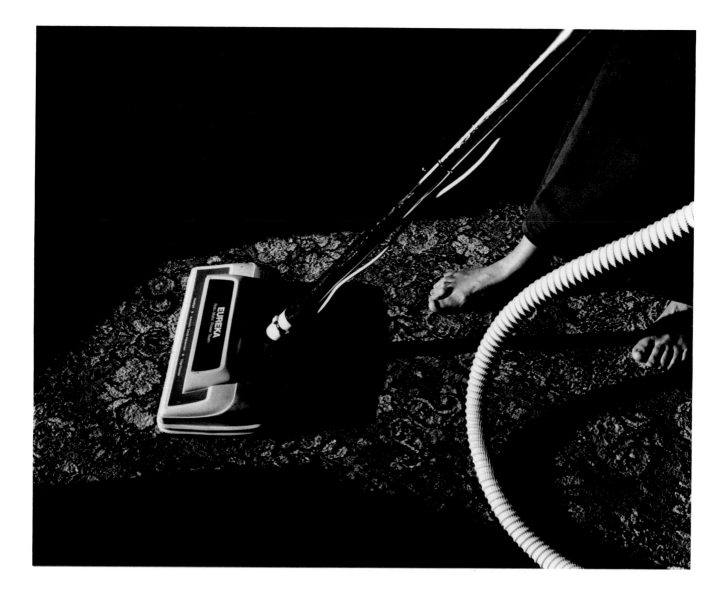

Nantucket

Deliberately, with great care and good reason, she left her husband and family, her job, the world itself and moved to an island for a season of solitude.

The time had come to hide and seek.

Alone, without friends or neighbors, she was free from smiling for the pleasure of others and found herself to be sufficient company. Her house was within sight and sound of the winter sea, which was a blessing, for gradually, unknowingly, she harmonized even her breathing with its rhythmic undulation. Eventually she heard inner as well as outer music and discovered that while listening, she temporarily ceased to be.

One stormy night the insistent wind tugged her attention away from Thoreau and made her yearn for something she could not name. Leaving the fireside she ventured out on to the wind-lashed dunes and saw the startling incandescent moon. Like some animal transfixed by headlights, she froze, staring wildly from the darkness, not knowing what would come next, yet certain that she was willing to die in order to see.

Hawks

She stood on the bluff and stared into the expanse of desert spread out like a relief map before her feet and wished she could fly or, better still, lose herself and become a bird, perhaps a redtailed hawk with a four-foot wing span and eyes that could detect rodents from five hundred feet above the earth. A creature capable of navigating wind currents without the aid of charts or numbers, immersed in life on the primal level, where instinct dictates the rules of the game.

What would it be like to live in the blood, outside of thought, clean and simple, always present, even to death?

Spirit can only inquire. It can never get a reply—outside of an echo. Spirit is—well, it is the drive to pile zero on zero endlessly in order to arrive at one.

Yukio Mishima, *Forbidden Colors*

I have known Tamarra Kaida for a dozen years, long enough so that although we are often separated for long periods by the necessities of our lives, the many things we have been to each other: professional colleagues, rivals in love, bearers and hearers of sweet and terrible secrets; and the spectrum of ways we have interacted: from easy openness to frosty withdrawal; and all the places and times we have talked: in autumn woods and summer kitchens, over the telephone and in offices, cars, airports and letters—all of these are now a lattice of memory, experience and expectation. We are friends. The effort to save the fragments and to piece them together meaningfully comes largely from Tamarra. Perhaps because her earliest recollections concern the desolation of rootlessness (she is an immigrant to this country, born in a displaced persons' camp), Tamarra connects to the world by creating and maintaining strong relationships with people.

Over the years, Tamarra has endeavored to transform what could have been a one-sided and insatiable longing to be part of things into a vested nurturance of her self and others. She is a good cook and a gracious hostess. She is an avid reader of art, psychology and fiction who sends these books to her friends. She is a teacher of great warmth who fosters her students' emotional as well as intellectual growth.

Underlying the nurturance are two allied social skills. For one, Tamarra is a storyteller. The fairy tale's broad characters and moral exemplum express her belief that even in this age of instant access and digitized reason, it is the credulous heart that guides human endeavor. And she is a listener. Close attention, an occasional astute question, elicit from Tamarra's companions—man, woman and child—detailed maps of their lives and timely reports of the climate there.

Tamarra is not a neutral observer, cloaked by the therapist's cool reserve. She takes to heart the child's frustration, the adolescent's confusion, the grown-up's battles won and lost. I know that it is painful for her, that the openness leaves her vulnerable to tides of emotion and emptiness. But the intuition that compels her embrace of human lives also has a refuge, a constructive and solitary mediation through the making of art. Gleaned from her delvings into the stations and progress and rituals of individuals, Tamarra's story and picture ensembles graph out, like the nervous lines of a cardiogram, the internal thud and sway of people confronting life's dilemmas.

Struggle is embedded in the architecture of the book. Structured by the double page spread, deepened by its careful sequences, the book is not a continuous narrative of its characters. Only occasionally does the picture on any right hand page make direct reference to the story on the left; their symbols are often unevenly intense, or even contradictory. Photographed in our own backyards and bedrooms, on the street corners of the cities where we live, at the beaches and parks we escape to, Tamarra's pictures are fictions set in contemporary time and place. The stories, on the other hand, chronicle the perennial sources of our anxiety: love, sexuality, aging, loss, and above all, loneliness. But the reverse is also true. Those places represent only the modern inflections in the ageless pursuit of shelter, sustenance and comfort, while the characters inhabiting them mutter argot and long to be au courant.

The diffusion, the uncertainty among words and pictures echoes the trials faced by the characters in the individual ensembles. In many of them, external sources challenge the reliability, even the reality, of internal experience. Not just the reports from television and newspapers, but their style, their very presence, invade our daily rounds, our midnight hours. In others, our dreams, hopes, fantasies and fears warp our perception of the world and scramble our ability to make sense of things. From this whirl of classic dichotomies: word/picture, mind/matter, reason/intuition, love/hate, life/death, whip the all too familiar tragedies of our modern confusion: self-deception, resignation, divorce, madness, suicide. Any of these is an oasis from the turmoil. None of them resolves it.

What are we to do then? accept the riddles? suffer them? transform them? Yes. That is the message of the book you hold in your hands. Were you taken in by the stories in the third, final sequence where the rifts melt, where a vision of peace calms the storm, where one fuses with Other? These are the events Tamarra and I thresh and savor in the kitchen, in our letters and on the phone. Each of us has strived for them, on our own, in groups, in therapies, courses and workshops of every stripe. Tamarra's word for it, when we're being serious, is spirit; mine is grace. We mean the rare magical clarity that in a moment and only for a moment has the power to shatter the mundane, cruel and terrifying length of days. Like a ghost story told in a darkened tent, it makes us shiver. When the chilling absurdity is finally too much, our name for it, in the shorthand of friendship, is hoogie-boogie, and we laugh until the tears come. Usually, then, for a while, we're quiet.

Susan E. Cohen
Rochester, NY, September 1988